SO-ASI-755

THE OLD DEMON

*This American classic
is presented without adaptation as part
of the Creative Classic series.*

THE OLD DEMON

PEARL S. BUCK

Illustrated by Sandra Higashi

Creative Education, Inc.
Mankato, Minnesota

28810337

Design: Neumeier Design Team
Editor: Ann Redpath
Biographical Sketch: Martha Fisk

Published by Creative Education, Inc.
123 South Broad Street, Mankato, Minnesota 56001

Copyright © 1982 by Creative Education, Inc. International copyrights reserved in all countries.
No part of this book may be reproduced in any form without written permission from the publisher.
Printed in the United States.

Acknowledgement: Reprinted by permission of Harold Ober Associates, Inc. Copyright © 1939,
1966 by Pearl S. Buck.

LIBRARY OF CONGRESS
CATALOG CARD NO.: 81-71040

 Buck, Pearl
  The old demon.

 Mankato, MN : Creative Education
 40 p.
 8112   811030

ISBN: 0-87191-828-5

To
the continuation of fine literature
for readers of all ages.

LD MRS. WANG KNEW
of course that there was a war. Everybody had known
for a long time that there was war going on and that
Japanese were killing Chinese. But still it was not real
and no more than hearsay since none of the Wangs had
been killed. The Village of Three Mile Wangs on the flat
banks of the Yellow River, which was old Mrs. Wang's
clan village, had never even seen a Japanese. This
was how they came to be talking about Japanese at all.

It was evening and early summer, and after her
supper Mrs. Wang had climbed the dike steps, as she
did every day, to see how high the river had risen. She
was much more afraid of the river than of the Japanese.
She knew what the river would do. And one by one the

villagers had followed her up the dike, and now they stood staring down at the malicious yellow water, curling along like a lot of snakes, and biting at the high dike banks. "I never saw it as high as this so early," Mrs. Wang said. She sat down on a bamboo stool that her grandson, Little Pig, had brought for her, and spat into the water.

"It's worse than the Japanese, this old devil of a river," Little Pig said recklessly.

"Fool!" Mrs. Wang said quickly. "The river god will hear you. Talk about something else."

So they had gone on talking about the Japanese. . . How, for instance, asked Wang, the baker, who was old Mrs. Wang's nephew twice removed, would they know the Japanese when they saw them?

Mrs. Wang at this point said positively, "You'll know them. I once saw a foreigner. He was taller than the eaves of my house and he had mud-colored hair and eyes the color of a fish's eyes. Anyone who does not look like us—that is a Japanese."

Everybody listened to her since she was the oldest woman in the village and whatever she said settled something.

Then Little Pig spoke up in his disconcerting way. "You can't see them, Grandmother. They hide up in the sky in airplanes."

Mrs. Wang did not answer immediately. Once she would have said positively, "I shall not believe in an airplane until I see it." But so many things had been true which she had not believed—the Empress, for instance, whom she had not believed dead, was dead. The Republic, again, she had not believed in because she did not know what it was. She still did not know, but they had said for a long time there had been one. So now she merely stared quietly about the dike where they all sat around her. It was very pleasant and cool, and she felt nothing mattered if the river did not rise to flood.

"I don't believe in the Japanese," she said flatly. They laughed at her a little, but no one spoke. Someone lit her pipe—it was Little Pig's wife, who was her favorite, and she smoked it.

"Sing, Little Pig!" someone called.

So Little Pig began to sing an old song in a high,

quavering voice, and old Mrs. Wang listened and forgot the Japanese. The evening was beautiful, the sky so clear and still that the willows overhanging the dike were reflected even in the muddy water. Everything was at peace. The thirty-odd houses which made up the village straggled along beneath them. Nothing could break this peace. After all, the Japanese were only human beings.

"I doubt those airplanes," she said mildly to Little Pig when he stopped singing.

But without answering her, he went on to another song.

Year in and year out she had spent the summer evenings like this on the dike. The first time she was seventeen and a bride, and her husband had shouted to her to come out of the house and up the dike, and she had come, blushing and twisting her hands together, to hide among the women while the men roared at her and made jokes about her. All the same, they had liked her. "A pretty piece of meat in your bowl," they had said to her husband. "Feet a trifle big," he had answered deprecatingly. But she could see he was pleased, and so gradually her shyness went away.

He, poor man, had been drowned in a flood when he was still young. And it had taken her years to get him prayed out of Buddhist purgatory. Finally she had grown tired of it, what with the child and the land all on her back, and so when the priest said coaxingly, "Another ten pieces of silver and he'll be out entirely," she asked, "What's he got in there yet?"

"Only his right hand," the priest said, encouraging her.

Well, then, her patience broke. Ten dollars! It would feed them for the winter. Besides, she had had to hire labor for her share of repairing the dike, too, so there would be no more floods.

"If it's only one hand, he can pull himself out," she said firmly.

She often wondered if he had, poor silly fellow. As like as not, she had often thought gloomily in the night, he was still lying there, waiting for her to do something about it. That was the sort of man he was. Well, some day, perhaps, when Little Pig's wife had had the first baby safely and she had a little extra, she might go back to finish him out of purgatory. There was no real hurry, though. . . .

"Grandmother, you must go in," Little Pig's wife's soft voice said. "There is a mist rising from the river now that the sun is gone."

"Yes, I suppose I must," old Mrs. Wang agreed. She gazed at the river a moment. That river—it was full of good and evil together. It would water the fields when it was curbed and checked, but then if an inch were allowed it, it crashed through like a roaring dragon. That was how her husband had been swept away— careless, he was, about his bit of the dike. He was always going to mend it, always going to pile more earth on top of it, and then in a night the river rose and broke through. He had run out of the house, and she had climbed on the roof with the child and had saved herself and it while he was drowned. Well, they had pushed the river back again behind its dikes, and it had stayed there this time. Every day she herself walked up and down the length of the dike for which the village was responsible and examined it. The men laughed and said, "If anything is wrong with the dikes, Granny will

She gazed at the river a moment. That river — it was full of good and evil together.

tell us."

It had never occurred to any of them to move the village away from the river. The Wangs had lived there for generations, and some had always escaped the floods and had fought the river more fiercely than ever afterward.

Little Pig suddenly stopped singing.

"The moon is coming up!" he cried. "That's not good. Airplanes come out on moonlight nights."

"Where do you learn all this about airplanes?" old Mrs. Wang exclaimed. "It is tiresome to me," she added, so severely that no one spoke. In this silence, leaning upon the arm of Little Pig's wife, she descended slowly the earthen steps which led down into the village, using her long pipe in the other hand as a walking stick. Behind her the villagers came down, one by one, to bed. No one moved before she did, but none stayed long after her.

And in her own bed at last, behind the blue cotton mosquito curtains which Little Pig's wife fastened securely, she fell peacefully asleep. She had lain awake a little while thinking about the Japanese and wondering why they wanted to fight. Only very coarse persons wanted wars. In her mind she saw large coarse persons. If they came one must wheedle them, she thought, invite them to drink tea, and explain to them, reasonably—only why should they come to a peaceful farming village . . . ?

So she was not in the least prepared for Little Pig's wife screaming at her that the Japanese had come. She sat up in bed muttering, "The teabowls—the tea—"

"Grandmother, there's no time!" Little Pig's wife screamed. "They're here—they're here!"

"Where?" old Mrs. Wang cried, now awake.

"In the sky!" Little Pig's wife wailed.

They had all run out at that, into the clear early dawn, and gazed up. There, like wild geese flying in autumn, were great birdlike shapes.

"But what are they?" old Mrs. Wang cried.

And then, like a silver egg dropping, something drifted straight down and fell at the far end of the village in a field. A fountain of earth flew up, and they all ran to see it. There was a hole thirty feet across, as big as a pond. They were so astonished they could not speak, and then, before anyone could say anything, another and another egg began to fall and everybody was running, running. . . .

Everybody, that is, but Mrs. Wang. When Little Pig's wife seized her hand to drag her along, old Mrs. Wang pulled away and sat down against the bank of the dike.

"I can't run," she remarked. "I haven't run in seventy years, since before my feet were bound. You go on. Where's Little Pig?" She looked around. Little Pig was already gone. "Like his grandfather," she re-marked, "always the first to run."

But Little Pig's wife would not leave her, not, that is, until old Mrs. Wang reminded her that it was her duty.

"If Little Pig is dead," she said, "then it is necessary that his son be born alive." And when the girl still hesitated, she struck at her gently with her pipe. "Go on—go on," she exclaimed.

So unwillingly, because now they could scarcely hear each other speak for the roar of the dipping planes, Little Pig's wife went on with the others.

And then, like a silver egg dropping, something drifted straight
down and fell at the far end of the village in a field.

By now, although only a few minutes had passed, the village was in ruins and the straw roofs and wooden beams were blazing. Everybody was gone. As they passed they had shrieked at old Mrs. Wang to come on, and she had called back pleasantly:

"I'm coming — I'm coming!"

But she did not go. She sat quite alone watching now what was an extraordinary spectacle. For soon other planes came, from where she did not know, but they attacked the first ones. The sun came up over the fields of ripened wheat, and in the clear summery air the planes wheeled and darted and spat at each other. When this was over, she thought, she would go back into the village and see if anything was left. Here and there a wall stood, supporting a roof. She could not see her own house from here. But she was not unused to war. Once bandits had looted their village, and houses had been burned then, too. Well, now it had happened again. Burning houses one could see often, but not this darting silvery shining battle in the air. She understood none of it — not what those things were, nor how they stayed up in the sky. She simply sat, growing hungry, and watching.

"I'd like to see one close," she said aloud. And at that moment, as though in answer, one of them pointed suddenly downward, and, wheeling and twisting as though it were wounded, it fell head down in a field which Little Pig had plowed only yesterday for soybeans. And in an instant the sky was empty again, and there was only this wounded thing on the ground and herself.

She hoisted herself carefully from the earth. At her age she need be afraid of nothing. She could, she decided, go and see what it was. So, leaning on her bamboo pipe, she made her way slowly across the fields. Behind her in the sudden stillness two or three village dogs appeared and followed, creeping close to her in their terror. When they drew near to the fallen plane, they barked furiously. Then she hit them with her pipe.

"Be quiet," she scolded, "there's already been noise enough to split my ears!"

She tapped the airplane.

"Metal," she told the dogs. "Silver, doubtless," she added. Melted up, it would make them all rich.

She walked around it, examining it closely. What made it fly? It seemed dead. Nothing moved or made a sound within it. Then, coming to the side to which it tipped, she saw a young man in it, slumped into a heap in a little seat. The dogs growled, but she struck at them again and they fell back.

"Are you dead?" she inquired politely.

The young man moved a little at her voice, but did not speak. She drew nearer and peered into the hole in which he sat. His side was bleeding.

"Wounded!" she exclaimed. She took his wrist. It was warm, but inert, and when she let it go, it dropped against the side of the hole. She stared at him. He had black hair and a dark skin like a Chinese and still he did not look like a Chinese.

He must be a Southerner, she thought. Well, the chief thing was, he was alive.

"You had better come out," she remarked. "I'll put some herb plaster on your side."

The young man muttered something dully.

"What did you say?" she asked. But he did not say it again.

I am still quite strong, she decided after a moment. So she reached in and seized him about the waist and pulled him out slowly, panting a good deal. Fortunately he was rather a little fellow and very light. When she had him on the ground, he seemed to find his feet; and he stood shakily and clung to her, and she held him up.

"Now if you can walk to my house," she said, "I'll see if it is there."

Then he said something, quite clearly. She listened and could not understand a word of it. She pulled away from him and stared.

"What's that?" she asked.

He pointed at the dogs. They were standing growling, their ruffs up. Then he spoke again, and as he spoke he crumpled to the ground. The dogs fell on him, so that she had to beat them off with her hands.

"Get away!" she shouted. "Who told you to kill him?"

And then, when they had slunk back, she heaved him somehow onto her back; and, trembling, half carrying, half pulling, she dragged him to the ruined village and laid him in the street while she went to find her house, taking the dogs with her.

Her house was quite gone. She found the place easily enough. This was where it should be, opposite the water gate into the dike. She had always watched that gate herself. Miraculous it was not injured now, nor was the dike broken. It would be easy enough to rebuild the house. Only, for the present, it was gone.

So she went back to the young man. He was lying as she had left him, propped against the dike, panting and very pale. He had opened his coat and he had a little bag from which he was taking out strips of cloth and a bottle of something. And again he spoke, and again she understood nothing. Then he made signs and she saw it was water he wanted, so she took up a broken pot from one of many blown about the street, and, going up the dike, she filled it with river water and brought it down again and washed his wound, and she tore off the strips he made from the rolls of bandaging. He knew how to put the cloth over the gaping wound and he made signs to her, and she followed these signs. All the time he was trying to tell her something, but she could understand nothing.

"You must be from the south, sir," she said. It was easy to see that he had eduction. He looked very clever. "I have heard your language is different from ours." She laughed a little to put him at his ease, but he only stared at her somberly with dull eyes. So she said brightly, "Now if I could find something for us to eat, it would be nice."

He did not answer. Indeed he lay back, panting still more heavily, and stared into space as though she had not spoken.

"You would be better with food," she went on. "And so would I," she added. She was beginning to feel unbearably hungry.

It occurred to her that in Wang, at the baker's shop there might be some bread. Even if it were dusty with fallen mortar, it would still be bread. She would go and see. But before she went she moved the soldier a little so that he lay in the edge of shadow cast by a willow tree that grew in the bank of the dike. Then she went to the baker's shop. The dogs were gone.

The baker's shop was, like everything else, in ruins. No one was there. At first she saw nothing but the mass of crumpled earthen walls. But then she remembered that the oven was just inside the door, and the door-frame still stood erect, supporting one end of the roof. She stood in this frame, and, running her hand in underneath the fallen roof inside, she felt the wooden cover of the iron caldron. Under this there might be steamed bread. She worked her arm delicately and carefully in. It took quite a long time, but, even so, clouds of lime and dust almost choked her. Nevertheless she was right. She squeezed her hand under the cover and felt the firm smooth skin of the big steamed bread rolls, and one by one she drew out four.

"It's hard to kill an old thing like me," she remarked cheerfully to no one, and she began to eat one of the rolls as she walked back. If she had a bit of garlic and a bowl of tea — but one couldn't have everything in these times.

It was at this moment that she heard voices. When she came in sight of the soldier, she saw surronding him a crowd of other soldiers, who had apparently come from nowhere. They were staring down at the wounded soldier, whose eyes were now closed.

"Where did you get this Japanese, Old Mother?" they shouted.

"What Japanese?" she asked, coming to them.

"This one!" they shouted.

"Is he a Japanese?" she cried in the greatest astonishment. "But he looks like us — his eyes are black, his skin —"

"Japanese!" one of them shouted at her.

"Well," she said quietly, "he dropped out of the sky."

"Give me that bread!" another shouted.

"Take it," she said, "all except this one for him."

"A Japanese monkey eat good bread?" the soldier shouted.

"I suppose he is hungry also," old Mrs. Wang replied. She began to dislike these men. But then, she had always disliked soldiers.

"I wish you would go away," she said. "What are you doing here? Our village has always been peaceful."

"It certainly looks very peaceful now," one of the men said, grinning, "as peaceful as a grave. Do you know who did that, Old Mother? The Japanese!"

"I suppose so," she agreed. Then she asked, "Why?

BLUE SPRINGS JUNIOR HIGH SCHOOL
LIBRARY

That's what I don't understand."

"Why? Because they want our land, that's why!"

"Our land!" she repeated. "Why, they can't have our land!"

"Never!" they shouted.

But all this time while they were talking and chewing the bread they had divided among themselves, they were watching the eastern horizon.

"Why do you keep looking east?" old Mrs. Wang now asked.

"The Japanese are coming from there," the man replied who had taken the bread.

"Are you running away from them?" she asked, surprised.

"There are only a handful of us," he said apologetically.

"We were left to guard a village — Pao An, in the country of — "

"I know that village," old Mrs. Wang interrupted. "You needn't tell me. I was a girl there. How is the old Pao who keeps the tea shop in the main street? He's my brother."

"Everybody is dead there," the man replied. "The Japanese have taken it—a great army of men came with their foreign guns and tanks, so what could we do?"

"Of course, only run," she agreed. Nevertheless she felt dazed and sick. So he was dead, that one brother she had left! She was now the last of her father's family.

But the soldiers were straggling away again leaving her alone.

"They'll be coming, those little black dwarfs," they were saying. "We'd best go on."

Nevertheless, one lingered a moment, the one who had taken the bread, to stare down at the young wounded man, who lay with his eyes shut, not having moved at all.

"Is he dead?" he inquired. Then, before Mrs. Wang could answer, he pulled a short knife out of his belt. "Dead or not, I'll give him a punch or two with this—"

But old Mrs. Wang pushed his arm away.

"No, you won't," she said with authority. "If he is dead, then there is no use in sending him into purgatory all in pieces. I am a good Buddhist myself."

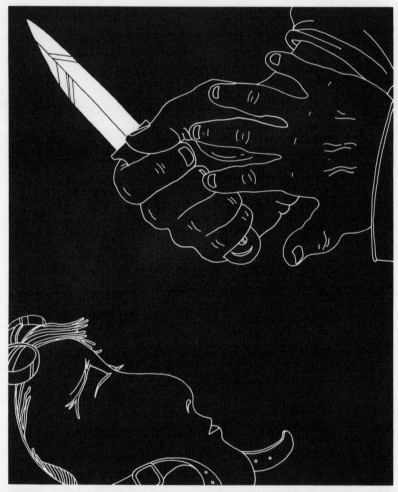

"Is he dead?" he inquired. Then, before Mrs. Wang could answer, he pulled a short knife out of his belt.

The man laughed. "Oh well, he is dead," he answered; and then, seeing his comrades already at a distance, he ran after them.

A Japanese, was he? Old Mrs. Wang, left alone with this inert figure, looked at him tentatively. He was very young, she could see, now that his eyes were closed. His hand, limp in unconsciousness, looked like a boy's hand, unformed and still growing. She felt his wrist but could discern no pulse. She leaned over him and held to his lips the half of her roll which she had not eaten.

"Eat," she said very loudly and distinctly. "Bread!"

But there was no answer. Evidently he was dead. He must have died while she was getting the bread out of the oven.

There was nothing to do then but to finish the bread herself. And when that was done, she wondered if she ought not to follow after Little Pig and his wife and all the villagers. The sun was mounting and it was growing hot. If she were going, she had better go. But first she would climb the dike and see what the direction was. They had gone straight west, and as far as eye could look westward was a great plain. She might even see a good-sized crowd miles away. Anyway, she could see the next village, and they might all be there.

So she climbed the dike slowly, getting very hot. There was a slight breeze on top of the dike and it felt good. She was shocked to see the river very near the top of the dike. Why, it has risen in the last hour!

"You old demon!" she said severely. Let the river god hear it if he liked. He was evil, that he was—so to threaten flood when there had been all this other trouble.

She stooped and bathed her cheeks and her wrists. The water was quite cold, as though with fresh rains somewhere. Then she stood up and gazed around her. To the west there was nothing except in the far distance the soldiers still half running, and beyond them the blur of the next village, which stood on a long rise of ground. She had better set out for that village. Doubtless Little Pig and his wife were there waiting for her.

Just as she was about to climb down and start out, she saw something on the eastern horizon. It was at first only an immense cloud of dust. But, as she stared at it, very quickly it became a lot of black dots and shining spots. Then she saw what it was. It was a lot of men — an army. Instantly she knew what army.

That's the Japanese, she thought. Yes, above them were the buzzing silver planes. They circled about, seeming to search for someone.

"I don't know who you're looking for," she muttered, "unless it's me and Little Pig and his wife. We're the only ones left. You've already killed my brother Pao."

She had almost forgotten that Pao was dead. Now she remembered it acutely. He had such a nice shop — always clean, and the tea good and the best meat dumplings to be had and the price always the same. Pao was a good man. Besides, what about his wife and his seven children? Doubtless they were all killed, too. Now these Japanese were looking for her. It occurred to her that on the dike she could easily be seen. So she clambered hastily down.

It was when she was about halfway down that she thought of the water gate. This old river — it had been a curse to them since time began. Why should it not make up a little now for all the wickedness it had done? It was plotting wickedness again, trying to steal over its banks. Well, why not? She wavered a moment. It was a pity, of course, that the young dead Japanese would be swept into the flood. He was a nice-looking boy, and she had saved him from being stabbed. It was not quite the same as saving his life, of course, but still it was a little the same. If he had been alive, he would have been saved. She went over to him and tugged at him until he lay well near the top of the bank. Then she went down again.

She knew perfectly how to open the water gate. Any child knew how to open the sluice for crops. But she knew also how to swing open the whole gate. The question was, could she open it quickly enough to get out of the way?

"I'm only one old woman," she muttered. She hesitated a second more. Well, it would be a pity not to see what sort of a baby Little Pig's wife would have, but one could not see everything. She had seen a great deal in this life. There was an end to what one could see, anyway.

She glanced again to the east. There were the Japanese coming across the plain. They were a long clear line of black, dotted with thousands of glittering points. If she opened this gate, the impetuous water would roar toward them, rushing into the plains, rolling into a wide lake, drowning them, maybe. Certainly they could not keep on marching nearer and nearer to her and to Little Pig and his wife who were waiting for her. Well, Little Pig and his wife—they would wonder about her—but they would never dream of this. It would make a good story—she would have enjoyed telling it.

She turned resolutely to the gate. Well, some people fought with airplanes and some with guns, but you could fight with a river, too, if it were a wicked one like this one. She wrenched out a huge wooden pin. It was slippery with silvery green moss. The rill of water burst into a strong jet. When she wrenched one more pin, the rest would give way themselves. She began pulling at it, and felt it slip a little from its hole.

I might be able to get myself out of purgatory with this, she thought, and maybe they'll let me have that old man of mine, too. What's a hand of his to all this? Then we'll—

The pin slipped away suddenly, and the gate burst flat against her and knocked her breath away. She had only time to gasp, to the river:

"Come on, you old demon!"

Then she felt it seize her and lift her up to the sky. It was beneath her and around her. It rolled her joyfully hither and thither, and then, holding her close and enfolded, it went rushing against the enemy.

Pearl S. Buck
1892-1973

PEARL BUCK said that she was as much Chinese as she was American. Born in West Virginia, her missionary parents took her to China a few months later.

Pearl grew up living right among the Chinese. Rather than live in a missionary compound, her parents chose a house among the native people, in a small city on the Yangtze River. Each day, Pearl's mother taught her school lessons in English, and in the afternoons her Chinese tutor came. When she was eighteen, she went to the United States to attend Randolph-Macon Woman's College in Virginia.

After graduating from college, she returned to China. Three years later she married John Lossing Buck, an American agricultural specialist. For the next five years she and her husband lived in a farming village in northern China. Pearl grew to love and admire the Chinese peasants and wanted to write about them. But she didn't have enough confidence yet to do it.

Then Pearl and her husband moved to Nanking, where they both taught at the University. There was much unrest in China at that time. In 1927 revolutionary armies invaded Nanking, and Pearl and her family had to flee for their lives.

Pearl's personal life created problems for her also. It was difficult for her to raise her mentally retarded daughter while she was trying to launch a writing career. Pearl soon found a way, however, to borrow some money and send her daughter to a special school for two years. This gave Pearl time to write. In a short time, her novel *The Good Earth* was published, and it brought her the Pulitzer Prize in 1932.

In 1934 she returned to the United States to live. She continued to write a steady stream of fiction, and won the Nobel Prize for Literature in 1938. She founded the East and West Association for the purpose of increasing understanding among the peoples of the world. Pearl adopted nine children of different nationalities and founded two agencies for the aid and adoption of Asian-American children. Her concern was always for children, "not because of a maternal instinct," she said, "for you know I am not a very maternal woman, but because children are the future."

BLUE SPRINGS JUNIOR HIGH SCHOOL
LIBRARY